Upstaged

other works by Jacques Jouet in English translation

Mountain R

Savage

Upstaged

A NOVEL BY **Jacques Jouet**

TRANSLATED AND WITH AN AFTERWORD BY
LELAND DE LA DURANTAYE

Dalkey Archive Press
Champaign and London

Originally published in French as *La Scène usurpée*
by Éditions du Rocher, 1997
Copyright © 2000 by Éditions du Rocher
Translation copyright © 2011 by Leland de la Durantaye
First edition, 2011
All rights reserved

Library of Congress Cataloging-in-Publication Data

Jouet, Jacques.
[Scène usurpée. English]
Upstaged / Jacques Jouet ; translated and with an afterword by Leland de la
Durantaye. -- 1st ed.
p. cm.
ISBN 978-1-56478-574-9 (pbk. : acid-free paper)
I. De la Durantaye, Leland. II. Title.
PQ2670.O926S3413 2011
843'.914--dc22
2011006262

Partially funded by the University of Illinois at Urbana-Champaign
and by a grant from the Illinois Arts Council, a state agency

Ouvrage publié avec le concours du Ministère
français chargé de la culture – Centre national du livre

This work has been published, in part, thanks to the
French Ministry of Culture – National Book Center

www.dalkeyarchive.com

Cover: design and composition by Danielle Dutton,
illustration by Nicholas Motte

Printed on permanent/durable acid-free paper
and bound in the United States of America

On Tuesday March 9th our eighth performance of *Going Out to the People*, written and directed by Marcel Flavy, was disrupted. Even now, it's extremely difficult to say whether this was unfortunate—either for us or for the audience. In any event, this disturbance was so artfully concealed from the public eye that the hallowed reputation of our national theater suffered no injury. Were it not for the professionalism of all involved—including, to be fair, the source of the disturbance himself—this would never have been possible.

5

There is something misleading in what I just wrote. What March 9th's audience saw was not actually *Going Out to the People*. Although they did not know it, although they could not know it, although there was no way for us to tell them, what they saw was far stranger.

For this to make any sense I need to begin at the beginning. Before I do, it is imperative that I stress that the following—indeed, somewhat contradictory—account was not written with the aim of assigning blame to any of the players in that night's drama. It should be remembered that these were professional artists violently shaken from their usual routines. There can be no doubt that for the duration of the crisis they performed to the best of their abilities. Taking sides for or against any of them would be not only inappropriate, it would be unfair. So as to be as absolutely explicit as possible: this document is offered with no other aim than the edification of a noble profession.

On the evening in question, the theater was filled to three-quarters of its full capacity (of eight hundred and fifty seats). In addition to the tickets sold, four complimentary press passes had been issued, two of which were redeemed. Alexandre Botsinas of *The Morning Republic* was to be found in his customary front-row seat, a notepad in his lap, the text of the play in hand. (I note these details as they were to prove not without importance.) Of the other journalist present nothing much need be said. Famed for his long critical naps, he was, in point of fact, actually asleep for the better part of the performance.

Act One proceeded as planned. Jean-François Ernu and Sylvestre Pascal-Bram breezed through its forty-five minutes in a mere forty-two—an acceleration that Marcel Flavy, the play's author and director, had demanded after a lethargic Sunday matinee performance. This picking up of the play's pace was made without notable cuts to the text, although a number of not-so-pregnant silences were filled. At this quickened rate, the dialogue between the head of state and his principal advisor was filled with new energy. When the President of the Republican Council decides to disguise himself as a common citizen for a night—to leave his palace incognito so as to take the pulse of his people, as it were— we sensed, for the first time, a genuine curiosity move through the theater. This seemed to bode well for what was to come. I made a note to myself: "*Pacing! Watch over it! It is the production's most vulnerable child!*" People who don't work in the theater tend not to to realize how the daily rhythm of performance works imperceptibly— and perniciously!—to slow delivery. Keeping watch over a play's tempo is therefore absolutely essential. For this reason it is as exciting as it is important to find ways to counter the eroding effects of performance.

During a brief pause between the first two acts (three minutes of soundtrack—not so much an intermission as a break for us to change the set), the two actors exchanged their favorable impressions of the performance with one of their colleagues, Annie Soulemenov, who does not go on until the beginning of Act Two—in the role of a prostitute. Annie shared their sense that things were going well and declared that she would do everything in her power to build upon this auspicious beginning.

The events this chronicle was undertaken to relate began in the second minute of the second act. Nicolas Boehlmer, preparing to smoke his last cigarette before going onstage, heard a knock at his dressing-room door. "Come in," he called out. He was to note later how difficult it was to deliver this unexpected line at a moment when he had already entered the imaginative universe of his character. In response to his invitation, a stranger entered—one wearing the same wig, makeup, and clothes as Boehlmer (the outfit—according to costume-designer Sylvie Plumkett—of "a careless intellectual"). As he watched this mirror of himself advance, he sensed that the catastrophe was already underway.

"What do you think you're doing he—?" Boehlmer exclaimed to his (significantly taller) double. He was not to have time to finish pronouncing the word "here," short though that word is. The stranger radiated a natural authority. He forced Boehlmer into a low chair with remarkable rapidity and agility, then gagged him, removed his threadbare jacket, suspenders, and pants, and tied him up. Boehlmer's wrists were forced beneath the chair and looped around his ankles, leaving him in a thoroughly uncomfortable position. He was in his underpants, bent forward, his head between his knees, one with his chair. Boehlmer said later that he had lacked the energy to put up even minimal resistance—a curious phenomena he attributed to the perfectly unthreatening authority of the intruder. Without wasting a moment, the man we came to call "the Usurper" tucked Boehlmer's jacket and pants under his arm, and, with surprising civility, apologized for his roughness. Boehlmer recalls the following phrase: "I am indeed taking a part of you, but you will soon find it returned unharmed. You have my word." The Usurper added: "In case this does not go without saying, I very much admire your work."

A moment later the stage manager called through the door that Boehlmer was due on stage in four minutes. The Usurper sipped from a bottle of mineral water, taking care to choose an unopened one, and left without further ceremony. Nicolas tried to call for help, but was able to produce no more than a muffled groan, impossible as it was for him to spit out the plastic bag held in his mouth by a red, white, and blue scarf—not red, white, and blue by chance.

It seems that the Usurper chose to take Boehlmer's costume with him when he left the dressing room in order to ensure that—in case the actor was freed too soon—Nicolas wouldn't be able to rush right out on stage. However, as it appears that the Usurper did not intend to extend his usurpation into Act Three, he let the costume fall in a darkened corner, leaving Boehlmer a small but real chance of finding it and finishing the role for which he had been cast.

Exactly as if he had been doing so for weeks, or, rather, as if he had actually become Boehlmer—the Usurper walked over and sat down next to Pauline Bensmaïla, the actress playing the role of the second prostitute—a role, it should be said, that is somewhat more developed than that of the first prostitute, played by Annie Soulemenov. Pauline was waiting for her entrance on a bench at the rear of the stage, next to the fire extinguisher. The blaze of red set against Pauline's dark dress was an arrestingly beautiful sight—one that, while not intended for the public, caught the sensitive eye of our house photographer, Gilbert Décoinçon. Gilbert was so struck by the image that, for once, he set aside his scruples and abandoned his cherished black-and-white so as to capture it in color. The result is a remarkable photograph, much sought after. But I digress. Back to Pauline. On her bench. Next to the fire extinguisher. And now the Usurper. She didn't notice anything out of the ordinary, though she did experience a moment of mild surprise when Boehlmer—that is, he who she believed to be Boehlmer—did not pat her shoulder as he had done during every performance since the dress rehearsal.

The moment she heard the phrase "loss of affection," pronounced in a loud voice by the President's counselor, Pauline was supposed to count off five *Nebuchadnezzar*'s, "Nebuchadnezzar 1," "Nebuchadnezzar 2," "Nebuchadnezzar 3," "Nebuchadnezzar 4," "Nebuchadnezzar 5," and then storm onto the stage. Each Nebuchadnezzar was to represent approximately one second. During rehearsals Pauline had observed that this particular name, if pronounced anywhere near correctly, and then followed by a number, took significantly longer than one second. She said she preferred *Nabucco*—"Nabucco 1," "Nabucco 2," and so on. Not wanting to give up his Babylonian sovereign for Giuseppe Verdi's, Flavy closed discussion of the matter by declaring that he did not care whether it was five chronometrically precise seconds or not. He wanted five *Nebuchadnezzars* and not one less. Changing tack, he went on to explain that the name should become "something like a mantra, the actress's mantra, a narrow path leading to her character."

Distracted by Boehlmer's absent gesture, Pauline got tripped up in her *Nebuchadnezzar*s and made an uneven entry, out of step with the evening's accelerated pace. Flavy noticed, Flavy grimaced. He thought of going up to the (impersonated) Boehlmer to offer a final bit of advice. As you might imagine, this is not the sort of thing that actors, as a rule, welcome. Strangely enough, however, they almost seem to welcome it from Marcel, "the debonair dictator," as Pacal-Bram calls him. Flavy is on record stating that it was at this moment he noticed that it was not Boehlmer who was waiting in the wings. He was so startled by this realization that he did not even try to prevent the Usurper from taking the stage. (And, after all, what good would it have done?) The entrance thus took place thirty seconds in advance, and quite jauntily—something we've chosen to adopt in subsequent performances.

Boehlmer's character is a rebel leader who had formerly been a brother-in-arms of the President of the Republican Council. Once in power, the President, ingratitude incarnate, stripped him of all rights and honors. Then he exiled him ("Be wary of he who crowns you"). But, unbeknownst to the President, the rebel (Boehlmer's character) disguised himself and remained in the capital—a flickering flame, the clandestine conscience of a dishonored Republic.

As soon as Flavy realized what had happened, what was happening, he reached for his walkie-talkie and issued an order, which it was my job to carry out. I was to find out what had happened to Boehlmer and whether he was in need of assistance—medical or otherwise. At that moment I was under the stage, having just released a fake rat that was made to traverse the boards by means of an invisible nylon string. I am the director's assistant—and, by that virtue, his factotum.

I am even sometimes called the *Factota*, which, linguistically speaking, is idiotic, but, well, there you go. I rushed backstage more than a little confused by the assignment I'd been given. I found Boehlmer's door locked. I knocked. There was no response. I pounded. Still no response. Pressing my ear to the keyhole, I finally made out something, something faint—a groan that was immediately drowned out by a fierce argument coming from onstage. At this point in Flavy's drama, the potentate and the pseudovagabond have not yet recognized one another, and are exchanging unpleasantries concerning the prostitute played by Soulemenov. (To be more precise, the President of the Council has not yet recognized his opponent, but the rebel *may* already have recognized his President. Although Flavy's text doesn't make this point clear, it would help explain the vehemence with which this man of the people counsels the prostitute against having anything to do with such a "dubious" personage as the disguised president.)

After some hesitation, and a few unsuccessful attempts at further communication via walkie-talkie, I rushed off to find Flavy. I was getting more and more anxious as I ran through one worst-case scenario after another. Once I located Flavy, a new problem presented itself. He was standing in the wings and didn't want to come with me. To watch an actor in profile is a special pleasure for the connoisseur, all the more so when that actor is unknown, unexpected—and perhaps acting for the first and last time. Such an actor is, as Flavy would later remark, a *hapax* of the stage. (A typical Flavian remark. *Hapax* means *unicum*.) I too, however, soon fell under the Usurper's spell. I stood rooted to the spot, fascinated by how he seemed instinctively to find the perfect intonations for every line, and yet through certain professional shortcomings botched several passages. In doing so, he completely inverted the hierarchy of values that six weeks of rehearsal had firmly established. The stranger had evidently seen our first performances—and, who knows, maybe even our rehearsals—as he not only knew his lines by heart, but every gesture, no matter how slight.

As the Usurper called out, "In virtue of my powers stripped," he reminded me of a gifted student of Léna Gomborska, or even of the early Léprant; one of the ones who didn't follow the former to Latin America or the latter to Pernand-Vergelesses. Though shaken from habits laboriously acquired, Jean-François Ernu and Sylvestre Pascal-Bram both adapted relatively well, *mutatis mutandis.* At moments, they even seemed concerned that they might not be holding their own against the newcomer. Think of all the things that must pass through an actor's mind when he or she is confronting something unprecedented onstage, and to which he or she must react in the unseen blink of an eye. Question after question. Has there been an accident? Was this planned? Is it a test? A destabilization exercise? An initiation ritual? A waking nightmare? But there's little time to wonder, and none to be shocked. You have to deal with what's before you, relying on your reflexes, and without the luxury of crossing your fingers.

In other words, the moment was filled to bursting with an extraordinary intensity. Compared with the preceding performances, this new incarnation of the fallen rebel was at once more touching and more fervent. What's more, he was both of these things *earlier* in the play. It was fascinating to observe. This is not meant as a criticism of Boehlmer's performance. He had only been following orders, after all—ones that reflected, from the very beginning, a conception of the role which he shared with the author and director of the play as little, apparently, as did his talented Usurper.

I was the first to emerge from this hypnotic state. I told Flavy that it was imperative he come to Boehlmer's aid, stressing that the man's life might be at stake. At last, and unwillingly, Marcel made for the spiral staircase. I let him go first. He has authorized me to report that he was *furious*—furious with Boehlmer for putting the performance at risk on precisely the evening when the feared critic Botsinas had chosen to come, armed, as ever, with his inflexible expectations. We entered Boehlmer's dressing room by force: Flavy kicked in the door, shattering the wood of its frame.

Boehlmer was doubled over, drooling a little. Flavy took hold of the front legs of the chair, lifting them roughly so as to raise the head of the still-confined man. No sooner had he done so than he began assailing the gagged actor with questions. I thought it prudent to intervene at this moment

and undid, not without difficulty, the patriotic
scarf tied around Boehlmer's head. He spit out the
plastic bag that had been stuffed into his mouth
and then vomited, making inarticulate noises as
he did so. Flavy grabbed a largish nail clipper
from a nearby makeup kit and began slashing
furiously at Boehlmer's bound wrists. Flavy is a
far cry from agile and I feared that he would only
succeed in wounding the forearms of the man
whom he hadn't ceased berating as I'd never seen
him berate anyone before. He called the—at last
liberated—Boehlmer an idiot and an imbecile.
If anything, however, Boehlmer was even more
infuriated than his abusive rescuer. Gradually
straightening his bent spine, he called Flavy inept, incompetent, a twit, a scumbag, a loser, and,
finally, a traitor to his class—the last of these a
surprisingly dated slur. He charged Flavy with being so incapable that he couldn't even guarantee
the security of his actors. Both men were to regret

this violent exchange, untempered by the least self-control and in no way reflecting the excellent working conditions to which the entire company had grown accustomed. I tried, at first without great success, to calm the two men.

Flavy continued to thunder away: "*For example*? You want to know what, *for example*, you could have done? You could have defended yourself! *For example*! Taken a swing at him! *For example*! That is, you *could* have, if you had the . . ." Flavy paused dramatically.

"The *what*? Go ahead! Say it!"

"You want me to say it?"

"Yeah, I want you to say it! Go ahead! Say it!"

"If you had *the balls*!"

"*The balls*? You want to see what I have the balls for? I'll show you what I have the balls for!"

Things were getting out of control.

"Okay, okay—" said Flavy with a placating gesture.

A distracted look came over Boehlmer's face. "*The stage!*" he cried. "What's happening on stage?"

"*On stage?* You want to know what's happening on stage?" Flavy regained the full force of his anger. "What's happening on stage is that you're fired! More than fired, you've been replaced! *Favorably* replaced!"

"What?" But Boehlmer didn't need to be told twice. He grabbed the tricolor scarf from me—I still don't know why—and charged out of the dressing room. It didn't take long for us to realize the catastrophe that would result from a near-naked Boehlmer rushing out onstage to attack his own character. We took off after him. Successive stampedes down the metal staircase that leads to the stage set it shaking. We heard the authoritarian "*shh!*" of the stage manager Jean-Pierre Capelier who, working the stage lights, looked more than a little unsettling in his black clothes, black facemask, and black gloves. Flavy managed to trip

Boehlmer just as he was about to run out on stage. He then completed his maneuver by hitting Boehlmer on the head with a wooden doorstop that happened to be within reach. I can bear witness to the fact that he apologized as he struck. The stage's side curtain reacted with a silent shudder.

The sounds of pursuit and capture had been heard by the actors but not the spectators—except perhaps those in the first rows. On stage the actors showed remarkable professionalism, discipline, and presence of mind in refraining from looking over at us. No sooner was Boehlmer unconscious than Flavy had me call a doctor. And then, within moments, he was back under the spell cast by the Usurper and the originality of what was transpiring on stage. The newest member of our troupe displayed a freshness and skill that calmed us in the face of disaster (though this was a calm mixed with cowardice). Given our other options, it seemed best to let things take their course, to continue our quiet study. Transfixed, as it were, by the silver lining of his misfortune, Flavy was rapidly taking notes, finding himself almost convinced—as he was to confess later—of the superiority of the Usurper's dramaturgical ideas. He even went so far as to consider offering him a place in the troupe, effective immediately.

Up to this point we'd all been hoping that the Usurper would, if nothing else, continue to follow the script. These hopes were soon dashed, however, as it became clear that the man playing the Republican Théodore Soufissis (the rebellious object of the aforementioned presidential ingratitude) had begun to deviate from the text of Flavy's play. By his own admission, Marcel Flavy is by no means a revolutionary writer, and does not personally share the radical theses of his character Soufissis, or even those of the other more or less Souffisian figures whom the president encounters during his adventure. Flavy's general intention was to advocate a certain tolerance without presenting the political theories of this or that individual in any detail. What he wanted to explore were the dramatic possibilities of the encounter between the two main characters—and to play upon the traces of past complicity resting beneath present resentment. Flavy's text is about a friendship confronted with an ambition that has become too great to share. Complicating Flavy's undertaking was the people's image of Théodore Soufissis—held up as he is in our Republic as a hero whose life was rich in accident and adventure, full of a Romanticism remote from any *Realpolitik.*

The Usurper, however, did not allow his character to slide down the slippery slope of outraged stoicism, as is called for in Flavy's play (a development very much in accord with what we know of the historical Soufissis). He kept to his lines, and yet at the same time began to rebel against it. At first this was done almost imperceptibly. Only gradually did his undermining of the text become clear. The Usurper succeeded thereby in slowly unsettling the usually effortless assurance of Jean-François Ernu, and, thereby, of the President. At first it was a discrete *clinamen*, a slight deviation in the orderly descent of textual atoms—a *not* absent in one place and slipped in somewhere else. Ernu soon found himself forced to embark on uncertain waters—responding to unexpected objections from his costar with only his own distant memories of Republican history as a guide (happily, he had brushed up a bit in preparation for his role). Despite his immense skill as an actor, it must be noted that Jean-François Ernu has never much liked—nor, indeed, excelled at—improvisation. It's a part of the profession that's always cost him enormous effort, and in which he never willingly engaged. The

Usurper began to speak a bit more slowly—less, it seemed, to leave Ernu more time for reflection than so that Botsinas would have time to turn the pages of the volume spread on his lap.

Before long it became obvious that Soufissis (or, rather, the current possessor of the role) had had enough. A ripple of uncertainty went through the troupe when he revealed the true identity of the disguised President a quarter of an hour earlier than was called for. He then let fall a scathingly ironic—and genuinely clever—turn of phrase, leading to a burst of laughter at the expense of the President's dignity. Remarkably, neither I nor any other member of the company was able to retain or reconstruct its precise phrasing. It was something to the effect that the once-rich cloak of sovereignty had been reduced to bits of moth-eaten something or other, riddled with holes, gnawed by worms . . . anyway, in bad shape. But said much better, so much better—I assure you.

In the concentrated space of an image, he gave a radical critique of a government as craven as it was inept.

Ernu, in the role of the offended President, hesitated between forced laughter and blind rage. He shot an imploring look in the direction of Sylvestre Pascal-Bram, who was playing his advisor, but who was, if anything, at even more of a loss than him, and thus incapable of offering impromptu counsel. Nevertheless, he did do something. Like the lieutenant who reacts to a dressing down from a captain by laying into a sergeant, Pascal-Bram launched into a vulgar tirade against Annie Soulemenov. Shown the way by his authoritarian finger, she exited through the garden and collapsed in tears onto a pile of old curtains the moment she was out of sight. Her final exit had taken place twenty minutes ahead of schedule, a tragedy for a young actress, augmented by the fact that the turn events had taken deprived her—as she was to repeat later on—of no fewer than four lines (three, by my count, but still).

Back on stage, Ernu issued a dignified appeal: "Théodore, you have never ceased to be my friend—" But no sooner had he begun than Théodore cut him off. What followed was a truly rousing speech that left a silence of rare intensity in its wake—such as rarely happens in the theater—broken finally by a salvo of applause, which, while impassioned, proved remarkably brief, as if those applauding suddenly felt they'd been too bold and so fell silent.

Because of its length and complexity, it wasn't possible for any of us to transcribe this speech. And, although pressing a single button would have sufficed, our sound technician did not record it. This is much to be regretted, but here too there can be no question of assigning blame—he had to be ready to receive orders from Flavy at any moment. Of course, this didn't prevent us from trying to reconstruct at least a few of the finer phrases from Théodore's speech. I recall one that hit its mark with particular force, when the President addressed his former friend with excessive familiarity and was rebuffed by Théodore's declaring that such terms were not appropriate. He was not, after all, speaking to a fellow prison guard.

"Lowly innocence faced with exalted tyranny—" This play on words—not at all in the style of Marcel Flavy—seemed to energize the Usurper. And it was, in fact, this line that served as a transition into an extended accusation centered around the following riddle: "What poor animal with thousands of heads moves on thousands of legs in the morning, half that many at midday, and on only two in the evening?"

The trenchant solution—given without leaving Ernu time to offer it up himself (presuming, of course, that he was capable of doing so)—was, "the

Republic!" The Republic began its day in Edenic democracy, found itself weakened by division at midday, and spent its evening on the despotic legs of a single individual. Soufissis specified that two legs were woefully insufficient to support the weight of thousands of heads and that they might come crashing down—and soon!—onto their inept porter.

This, at last, proved too much for Jean-François Ernu. No longer able to find the energy to respond, and as if fulfilling his opponent's riddling prophecy, he chose, of his own accord, to descend the winding stair of unconsciousness. After acting out a dawning stupefaction dosed with a measure of belatedly realized guilt, he succumbed to the Usurper's verbal blow. He put his hand on his heart and, without word, complaint, or cry, slid to the floor, KO'd, theatrically dead.

At this moment, Sylvestre Pascal-Bram, in the role of advisor, threw himself bravely into the breach, improvising a declaration of everlasting fidelity to his fallen master. The Usurper seemed to abandon the rigid mantle of moral superiority and congratulated Pascal-Bram—not without irony—on his fidelity. Nevertheless, the rebel then enjoined the deputy to depart immediately, so as to leave him alone with this "fallen nothing." Soufissis told the audience that he would now do the only thing one could do with such a President— one who absents himself when most needed. He, Théodore, was going to eat him. Immediately. Preferably without witnesses. Soufissis removed a switchblade from his pocket, which swung open with a sinister click. Leaving his scruples on stage, Sylvestre Pascal-Bram exited.

Soufissis's repetition of the phrase, "I'm going to eat him," spoken while baring his teeth and brandishing his knife, coupled with the inert body lying in front of him, was less ridiculous than frankly unsettling. Strange as it might seem to heads and hearts that have since cooled, *many* of those present who were able to gauge the liberties already taken now assumed the threat was somehow real. It even occurred to me for a moment that the stranger was perhaps, in real life, the sworn enemy of Jean-François Ernu and had chosen to take advantage of this situation to conclude his dark business.

Left alone with what remained of the President, Théodore Soufissis cast a long, contemptuous look at the inert body. He showed, however, no immediate intention of acting out his threat. Instead, he launched into a monologue on how Power—with a capital P—infects generosity, comparing it to a particularly inviting but poisonous mushroom. Then, as if suddenly aware of his excessive grandiloquence, he gave his metaphorical mushroom more concrete form, speaking of derisory *lycoperdons*, also known as puffballs, an image meant to denounce, he said, "power with a little—*very* little—*p.*" Here and elsewhere, the Usurper did not shy away from authorial inter-jections—comments that seemed less appropriate to his character than to some unseen playwright. While the real usurped author didn't especially care for these digressions, they seemed to find favor with the audience.

Backstage, our unease had settled a bit. Our inactivity approached stasis. Flavy was too fascinated to give clear orders, I myself was cowed by how enthralled Flavy had become, Boehlmer was unconscious, and Annie Soulemenov had disappeared. The stage manager retained his unflagging cool and customary efficiency, but wouldn't venture beyond the bounds of his pre-assigned responsibilities—which, all things considered, was probably for the best, since this, at least, didn't add to the already very significant disorder. Anxious calls were coming from the control booth, to which Flavy replied, "Nobody panic! Nobody do anything! Just take care of the lighting!'"

But the lighting was not enough.

Ultimately, it was Pauline who saved the day. The extraordinary manner in which she did so, however, requires some explanation. And a few supplementary details. When first trying on her costume, she had voiced strong reservations concerning the dress created for her by Sylvie Plumkett, and which—she felt—failed to take sufficient account, and advantage, of her legs. She was heard to remark that a costume designer could not dress all her actresses as though they shared the designer's own figure—a remark that Ms. Plumkett, as you might imagine, did not take at all well. In particular, Pauline objected to two elements that she claimed sapped her character's strength—her black stockings, and the excessive length of her skirt (which was, I should say, not all that long). On this evening, however, thanks to the fact that nothing else was going according to plan, and with a decisiveness that suggested premeditation, Pauline removed her stockings and hitched up her skirt a good eight inches (from the waist, that is: rolling the skirt and fixing it with paperclips). The result was that her diminutive backside was significantly more present—although still, strictly speaking, covered—and her long legs were, as even Flavy conceded, considerably leggier.

Having effected these modifications, Pauline marched onto the stage without further ado, interrupting the Usurper's monologue and perhaps even believing that she was saving Ernu from being devoured. A wave of emotion went through the theater. Pauline was stunning. Flavy, however, had one reservation. He felt that, because of the excessive pallor of her legs, Pauline was the only thing one could see on stage. "She needed *something*. Makeup. Or a tan. They looked like ivory, right off an elephant, in that light. Like ice!" he was to blurt out later.

Coldness, however, wasn't the impression made on the stranger, who didn't have to be asked twice to attend to the newly arrived streetwalker. What happened next was exceptional, extraordinary, having nothing—and I do mean nothing—to do with Flavy's play. Théodore—or the Usurper, since at this point we really were in no position to say where one stopped and the other started—put his hand into his pocket and produced a handful of bills (large denominations). He then slid them, with a passion bordering on violence, into the waistband of the prostitute—or Pauline, we were now just as much at sea with her as with him. She found herself doubly surprised: first by his impulsive gesture, and then by the fact it didn't bother her.

The bills proved genuine, as did the mutual attraction. The audience responded with another silence of the sort that actors don't soon forget.

With the scene on stage growing more intimate by the minute, Flavy got on the line with the control booth and told them to get ready for a blackout with dropped curtain. Théodore took Pauline into his arms for an embrace that, if it wasn't actually charged with intense eroticism, certainly showed great skill in its imitation. Darkness came and the curtain fell as the Usurper lowered the black garter he had just compared, elegantly, to a violin bow. Though indeed unprecedented, the end of the act didn't come across as especially abrupt, and was met with a long round of applause.

This was not, however, a moment for congratulations. Flavy cried out, "Meeting! Meeting! Everybody backstage!" We had two minutes.

"Where is he? He has to go back on! There's no other way!"

We looked everywhere for the Usurper, but he was gone. He had disappeared into the darkness.

In an old-fashioned theater of that size there are more hiding places than you can count. Besides which, he could even have escaped out into the audience, for all we knew, and sat down without being seen by the ushers, since they'd all left to man the coat check. One (totally insufficient) minute was spent in a wild search for the Usurper, with each of us authorized to offer him a complete amnesty on the condition that he finish the play—whatever the price to be paid by Flavy's text. If pressed, we were told to offer him monetary compensation and even a contract for a role in Flavy's next play, which he was already working on.

The Usurper, however, was nowhere to be found. What's more, he wasn't the only one. Like him—and, perhaps, *with* him—Pauline had disappeared too, though this was of comparatively minor importance given that she wasn't in the final act. It was then that Boehlmer—having recently regained consciousness, if not costume—appeared in underwear and socks, rubbing his head with the red, white, and blue gag that was still in his hand. At his request, the doctor administered a stimulant under the pretext that it was imperative he continue—or, more accurately, *begin*—to act. He had, however, nothing to wear. Things weren't getting any easier, and the clock was ticking.

As the stagehands had no instructions to the contrary, they proceeded as though nothing were amiss and during the brief intermission moved the palace décor familiar from Act One back on stage. The real problem was that Boehlmer's role—that of Théodore Soufissis—was not at an end. During a reception at the Presidential palace commemorating the reconciliation of the two main characters, he was meant to take his own life in the presence of his former friend. Though Boehlmer had now managed to revive the fury that had preceded the blow to his head, Jean-François Ernu's energy level, in the wake of his simulated faint, had now plummeted in the opposite direction. He did not wish to continue—not under any circumstances—and was easily persuaded by Boehlmer to cede the role of the President. Certain that the Usurper would reappear in Act Three to complete his dramatic pronunciamento, Boehlmer intended to avenge himself.

At that moment, Annie Soulemenov, with no tears left to shed, had been making her way back to the dressing rooms; en route, she had discovered the costume of Boehlmer-Soufissis, which she now carried back to her colleagues as though it were the Shroud of Turin.

"What the fuck do you want me to do with that?" asked Flavy, before coming to his senses and thanking her.

"This could end badly," muttered Jean-Pierre Capelier.

If Boehlmer was going to put on Ernu's costume and insist with such tenacity on playing the President, Pascal-Bram said he wanted no part of it. Fixated on Botsinas and the fact that the crowd had reacted so well to the preceding act, Flavy saw matters in a different light: "The show must go on," he said. "The show *must go on*! An actor's calling is sacred! So long as there's an audience, we act! There's an audience out there, isn't there? So we're going to act!"

Jean-Pierre Capelier and myself, having been dispatched to find the Usurper, were now returning to the fold empty-handed. Looking to teach by example, Flavy took the Soufissis costume and quickly put it on. Capelier then called the control booth, where, alas, they misinterpreted this call as the signal to lift the curtain. And suddenly there was light. On an empty stage.

Boehlmer strode out as the President still disguised as a man of the people (we had forgotten about the character's between-act costume change), with the red, white, and blue handkerchief now stuffed into his coat pocket. He was followed by a Sylvestre Pascal-Bram who moved as though mounting a scaffold. The audience showed no sign of recognizing that a change in cast had occurred. Clothes make the man. At least some of the time.

Act Three picked up largely as it was written. Boehlmer knew the role of the President—one he had always secretly longed to play—more or less by heart. The reconciliation between the President and Soufissis was announced. Considering the far more radical role Soufissis had played in the preceding act—for most of which Boehlmer had been unconscious—it fell to Pascal-Bram, as the President's advisor, to express his reservations concerning a reconciliation on live television. But Boehlmer, hungry as he was for vengeance, held firm and gave the order to summon the cameraman (played by myself). I entered with my video camera and began discretely preparing my establishing shots.

At the precise moment when Flavy made his entrance as Théodore, a tiny black undergarment drifted down from the rafters. I distinctly saw Flavy turn pale—from jealousy? It wasn't difficult to deduce that the lovebirds must have reached the loft via a narrow ladder that the Usurper had doubtless planned on employing for his escape, but which Pauline, in her high heels, wasn't likely to have had an easy time with. It was, however, too late to act on this realization. For her part, Pauline later maintained that she'd never been up in the rafters, and had long since taken refuge in her dressing room. Alone. Did we believe her? No. Why not? Pauline's testimony wasn't espe-cially rich in detail, and each time I went back to her for clarifications she responded with nothing more than an immense sadness. I never had the heart to push very hard. In any event, whether or not anything scandalous was going on in those dim upper reaches, we had to keep our eyes on the stage. There were a few laughs in response to the fall of the garment, though from where the audience was sitting they couldn't possibly have seen that what had drifted down was lingerie.

When Boehlmer saw Flavy enter, was he still expecting the return of the Usurper? Impossible to say. Whatever his expectations, he wasted no time, seeming to relish the opportunity to rough Théodore up a little, at least verbally, even if it couldn't have escaped his notice that it was Flavy and not the Usurper in the role. Having taken the Usurper's place, Flavy began to pay his price. Or perhaps not. Unlike Jean-François Ernu, Boehlmer excelled at the art of improvisation, and was far and away the best at it in our troupe. Boehlmer began to harangue his special guest in a far more vulgar fashion than would be expected from the mouth of a President—even an angry one. Without the means to stem the tide of insults breaking over him, Flavy suffered in silence.

In my role as camerawoman needing to capture a few images of incontestable goodwill, I thought it best to interrupt Boehlmer with a reminder of what it was I was doing there. He marched over, took me by the scruff of the neck, and dragged me offstage, voicing, as he went, his contempt for the press in general, and television in particular. I think it's worth noting here that when things start to go wrong, the first reaction always seems to be to usher all the women offstage. Curious. Or maybe not so curious. In any event, Flavy used this interruption to return to the letter of his text, launching with great conviction into a long monologue, one of the finest and most moving in his play:

"This carpet with its rich wool and ornate design is thirsty, I say, thirsty! . . . I have come to seal an impossible pact . . . I will replace it with an impossible act . . ." And so on.

In response, Boehlmer gave voice to all the accusations and anger that he had swept under his own carpet since the first moments of his confinement, and, for that matter, since the first day of rehearsals, when Flavy had distributed the roles without regard for his actors' preferences—including, of course, Boehlmer's.

The confrontation between the two men had now reached a state of equilibrium: each character equally ready, willing, and able to respond to the other's accusations. A moment of respite. This created, however, a problem for the plot: it wasn't going anywhere. The actors were like two rams, horns locked, neither giving an inch. Flavy's Soufissis seemed to have become decidedly less suicidal, while Boehlmer's President was openly gloating over his right to banish this burdensome witness to the ways he had used his absolute power.

The scene went on, and on, seeming condemned to run aground in the sands of inactivity. The audience continued to wait—expecting, at least vaguely, the tragic end of Théodore Soufissis. When two groups of spectators rose and left the theater, however, Boehlmer realized where things were headed and changed course. He declared to Soufissis that as the promised reconciliation was not to take place: one of them must die. Flavy grabbed this verbal ball on the fly and returned to his text, announcing his refusal of any egalitarian duel and his intention of unilaterally staining the Presidential carpet with blood. Unfortunately, the pistol that was normally in the pocket of Boehlmer's costume had disappeared, falling out when Annie Soulemenov had rushed back toward the stage. What was Flavy to do?

After a long diatribe ridiculing the pretence of someone who grandly announces their imminent suicide only to realize they've forgotten to

procure the instrument with which to perform it,
Boehlmer offered a solution to this dramaturgical problem: he moved to the large presidential
desk and opened a drawer. A simple glance into
the (empty) drawer sufficed for the audience to
deduce that he was looking at a weapon. Flavy
approached, thrust his hand into the drawer, and
withdrew it with great energy while taking care
to turn away from the audience. Then he thrust
the phantom knife into his stomach. As hara-kiris
go, it wasn't great, but it sufficed. Bent forward,
Flavy tottered toward the vast carpet. After a last
gasp of pain, he collapsed onto it, expiring with
his nose buried in the wool's deep pile. Unexpect-
edly, this got a huge laugh—laughter, however,
that somehow managed not to seem mocking.
The President advanced to the edge of the stage,
apparently fixing the audience with his stare—
though, in actual fact, he was trying to stare down
the stage manager high above, who was asking

himself when he should cut the lights. Boehlmer's look was unequivocal: you will do so only after my final line! He let loose a sardonic cackle that instantly quieted the audience's laughter. Then he added, icily: "Never again!"

Black. Curtain. Immediate applause. Hallelujah.

You know the feeling. The nightmare is over. Land-ho. Salvation. The end of an hour of chaos for an exhausted teacher—That happened to me once when I taught preschool. It was horrible. But, at last, darkness. Though an audience often manifests relief by rushing for the exits, they treated us to round after round of warm, enthusiastic applause. We responded unreservedly, with much smiling and bowing, as if we'd just pulled off *King Lear* without a single misplaced iamb or unshed tear. During the third round of applause there was a noticeable intensification as Pauline joined us, a dazed smile on her face. Her black stockings were on again. And then, during the fifth round of applause, the Usurper appeared behind us. We didn't see him. When we broke ranks, he rushed towards Pauline, gallantly presenting her with a red rose. This done, he leapt over the footlights and into the audience, thereby clearing both a visible and an invisible hurdle. The audience reacted with a final explosion of applause as the theater went dark. He disappeared into the crowd, which was already moving toward the exits.

We never saw him again.

Before concluding, and at the relatively disinterested request of Marcel Flavy, I append to my report the complete text of Alexandre Botsinas's review, published in *The Morning Republic* on the Monday following our performance. After the end of the play, the critic did not elect to stay and have a drink with us, as is his custom.

"That there," said Jean-Pierre Capelier to me, "is a paralyzed critic. Look at him, all wrapped up in his coat as though someone's been bludgeoning him—without intermission!—for the past two hours" (normally an hour and forty minutes, but we went over a bit).

"Exhausted," I acknowledged.

"And something tells me that he isn't going to keep that exhaustion to himself," added Flavy with a bitter smile, which he then couldn't manage to relax.

Botsinas surprised us, however. And, as you can judge for yourself, agreeably:

>*Going Out to the People*, a play in three acts, written and directed by Marcel Flavy on National Stage Seven, with Pauline Bensmaïla, Annette Nois, Annie Soulemenov, Sylvestre Pascal-Bram, Jean-François Ernu, Nicolas Boehlmer. Scenery and costumes:

Sylvie Plumkett. Lighting: Jean Sachs and Jean-Pierre Capelier.

A False Departure Followed by a Real Return . . .

—unless it would be better to say, "A not-quite-false departure followed by a not-quite-real return." Marcel Flavy has offered us a remarkable new play—a historical drama that is bold in subject and artful in execution. It should be seen by everyone who has not completely given up on modern theater.

In these days when so many are seeking to foster interest in our history among the younger generations, Marcel Flavy—talented refugee first from the Lounia Company and then from Paul Batteux's troupe (which explains much)—offers us a splendid surprise. In three acts lasting two hours and depicting twenty-four hours of national history, we witness the reunion between the legendary "Real-President" of the preceding century, as Alcover calls him in *Portraits in Vitriol*, and the man who was his dearest friend during the period of his ascension and his bitterest enemy once his power became absolute. The visit to the people that gives the play its title also drives its plot: from the president's decision to disguise himself for a wild night with his subjects to the sobering day after. Everything revolves around the encounter between the two men—as if Fidel Castro were to run into Che in a sordid back alley in Havana.

In this face-off there is some first-rate verbal jousting and an extremely original use of dramatic hesitation. It was as if the

This play is taxing, tiring. I won't pretend otherwise. But it is these things for good reason, and I see signs in it of a new aesthetic, one that is still in its infancy. The play is not a manifesto, but it does offer a program—and one worth following. I always leave the theater with a migraine, but not always the same one. There is the bad migraine that comes from boredom, but there is also the good migraine, the migraine of open, probing, questioning theater. I hardly need to specify that it was with the latter—and, indeed, one of extraordinary intensity—with which I left the theater on this evening.

I shall conclude, as ever, with the potentially fatal detail—but, in this case, a detail that is, happily, easy to correct. It is possible from time to time to see a white face gazing through the curtain—something that is simply unacceptable on a national stage. Not to mention the rags occasionally falling from the rafters.

Alexandre Botsinas

Yes, the article pleased us all. Flavy postponed his inevitable ideological corrections of Botsinas's remarks to a later date so as not to lessen our relief or dampen our joy. First and foremost we needed to recover a measure of calm after such a trying experience. We were in something like post-operative shock. Sylvestre Pascal-Bram told us later that when he sat down in front of his dressing room mirror to remove his makeup, he said both *to* and *of* himself, "And that bit's real, right?" Annie Soulemenov told us that she was changing her profession, effective immediately. And the moment he sat down again in that chair of his, now so full of sinister associations, Nicolas Boehlmer burst into tears.

Such depressive and depressing occurrences hardly augur well for a troupe with an additional twenty-five performances ahead of it—not to mention the inevitable tour to follow. Oh, and—I'd almost forgotten—at least four matinee performances for schoolchildren.

When Capelier proposed that we request some security personnel, at least for the next performance, he was immediately shouted down: "No cop sets foot in this theater!" one of us said. "What are we actually risking?" asked another. And at that moment we felt a unanimous warmth—especially intense among the actors—well up for our Usurper, and we all gave voice to it. Even Boehlmer couldn't tell his dressing-room story without a note of admiration, even something like gratitude, creeping into his voice. (It's common for victims to develop a curious empathy, even camaraderie, with their captors.)

Eventually, our performances returned more or less to normal, though not without difficulty. It was painful not to be able to retain, not to be able to reproduce, all the wonderful touches of that one ephemeral evening. And it wouldn't be far from the truth to say that each of us, the moment before making his or her entrance, would have welcomed the opportunity to be captured and confined—put out of commission by a gentleman thief who'd now become the subject of so many dreams and desires. (It bears noting that Pauline isn't necessarily the most melancholy of our troupe in this regard.)

There is, however, one last question we need to address before closing the book on this case, before I conclude my report: Who was the Usurper? The answer is that we will probably never know. No one has claimed responsibility for his actions. We haven't filed charges.

But actually, there are hundreds of questions remaining. What would have happened if Pauline hadn't arrived to deflect matters? Would the Usurper have beaten the tyrant to a pulp? Had he done so, would this have meant that his actions amounted to a political statement? And, if so, would his message have been unambiguous enough to be attributable to a particular movement? Was his invasion not a failure, in the end, given that he ensured the President would have the last word? And why didn't the Usurper include Act Three in his calculations? Or did he, and Pauline was the glitch in his system? And yet, who's to say that the Usurper wasn't just a simple spectator who'd seen our earlier performances, and who had fallen in love with Pauline—a hypothesis supported by the clearly premeditated rose? And yet, if this were the case, why hasn't he sought her out since? Isn't it more likely that he was an actor, that he was one of our own? Perhaps he had a grudge to settle with our company. Or maybe he wanted to test us? But if that's the case—if you're reading this—come see us! We'll welcome you with open arms. Perhaps this account might even serve to convince you to come back to us. You presented us with a formidable challenge, and we rose to the occasion. Isn't that worth something?

But if the Usurper was a man of the theater, someone wishing us ill, someone trying to damage our reputation, to lower our standing at a time when funding has become so scarce and professional discord so rampant, he should have done things very differently—it would have been so easy to simply bring the entire performance to a halt! In short, none of the obvious explanations fit. Every one of them is contradicted by one detail or another.

Jean-François Ernu, however, has advanced a subtler hypothesis: that this fake Soufissis was actually a Soufissis in real life as well—someone who had experienced exactly that sort of violated friendship—not with a President, certainly, but with, say, a cabinet minister, like the one in attendance that very evening, and who, by the way, instead of coming backstage to congratulate us, fled the theater as soon as the show was over. Flavy has tried to find out what Her Honor thought of the performance, but his inquiries were all in vain. No comment.

And if we look farther afield? Could that evening have been the work of an agent provocateur? A specialist in such "republican" acts? Was it, in fact, a tiny libertarian coup? An almost imperceptible piece of civil disobedience? Sure, anything's possible, of course—but, then, who was our infiltrator? Always and again: *who*? Wouldn't that sort of man have wanted to reveal himself, wouldn't he want publicity, to be put to trial, wouldn't he want as much attention as possible for his daring deeds? Silence doesn't fit the profile.

There is one other outlandish hypothesis. The best, in fact. I dare you to do better. What if our

Usurper was none other than the President himself—like Nero slipping into the roles of the great
tragedians? Yes, our President himself, so well
known for his unpredictability, deciding to act
out his own outing as a tyrant to his people! But,
then, the Usurper was much taller than our President. And, after all, we would have recognized
him. And, again, *why*?

As I said, it's exceedingly unlikely that we'll ever
find answers to our questions. The theater, for its
part, continues (because nothing stops it). The
smart money is on our taking what we learned
that night and parleying it into a future success.

The day after that fateful night—the one Boehlmer now simply calls "The Evening," with
those capital letters he's so good at pronouncing—Flavy took us all—including the entire production team—out to lunch. It was on this occasion that he asked me to write this account of the
events. He reserved a table for eleven, well aware

that there were only ten of us. We ate and drank in the presence of an empty chair. Marcel paused a moment before raising his glass for a toast, saying, at last, "Viewed as a performance, it wasn't too bad. In fact, I think it was one of our best."

Afterword
The Republic of Jacques Jouet

For readers unfamiliar with Jacques Jouet's vast oeuvre, a few words on two topics are in order. The first of these is his *Republic,* the second its *constraints.*

Since the violent fall of its monarchy in 1789, France has been committed to the idea of the republic. So much so that in this interval it has known no fewer than five republics—which it is the joy and sorrow of French schoolchildren to enumerate and explicate. Jouet, formerly a French schoolchild, is the author of a series of works to which he has given the title *La Répub-lique roman*. The books that make up that grow-ing republic vary widely in form, content, and length. What they share is a republican ardor of a special sort.

Jouet's literary productions are ample, diverse, and extend, in fact, beyond his Republic. He be-gan as a poet and continues as one, most monu-mentally in *Navet, linge, oeil-de-vieux* (Turnip, Linen, Oeil-de-Vieux), a collection of verse—in a day when volumes of poetry tend ever more towards brevity—of more than nine hundred pages. Jouet is a practicing playwright and his dramas have been staged all over the world—from Paris to Ouagadougou. He is the author of a lexicographical work cataloging French figures of speech that involve parts of the body (of which there are more than a few).[1] All told, he is today

---

1   *Les mots du corps dans les expressions de la langue française.* (Paris: Larousse, 1990).

the author of more than fifty books spanning the genres of poetry, drama, criticism, fiction, and biography. And in that impressive production *La République roman* occupies a special place.

To date, the Republic consists of thirty-seven works of shorter and longer fiction (Jouet insists that he doesn't write novellas, just shorter and longer novels). It began in 1994 with *Le Directeur du Musée des cadeaux des chefs d'Etat de l'étranger* (The Director of the Museum of Gifts from Foreign Heads of State) and took hold with his next book—and his first to be translated into English—*Mountain R*, in 1996.[2] Since then it has been populated by works of all sorts—from, to pick the productions of a single year, the slim and symmetrical *Annette et l'Etna* to the gargantuan and sprawling *La République de Mek-Ouyes* (both 2001).

---

2   Translated by Brian Evenson for Dalkey Archive Press in 2004.

Jacques Jouet is not the first Frenchman to create such a fictional republic. In July of 1842, Honoré de Balzac, half-dead from caffeine abuse, finished his *Comédie Humaine*. The inspiration for his title was not humble. It had a precedent in another comedy—Dante's divine one. Dante, in fact, never referred to his work as anything other than as his *"Commedia"*; the *"Divina"* came from a different hand.[3] Balzac, however, did not know this and did not need to. His concern was with this world and the life led in France's new republic. In the preface he wrote for a comedy which spanned some ninety works and featured more than two thousand characters, he praises the wonders of electricity, laments that Walter Scott had not been born Catholic, and announces that his great work was written to serve as a history of morals and manners for France's young republic. Whereas

---

3   Though an illustrious one—that of Boccaccio.

Dante wrote an allegory of the *divine* side of life, Balzac aspired to write an account of its *human* one. Were Jacques Jouet not so modest a writer, he might have titled his series of works *The Republican Comedy*, as *La République roman* has a similar aspiration—to offer a comedy both light and dark, sinister and innocent, of this world and its republics.

Jouet has noted that he began his *République roman* "in thematic terms" with *topoi* such as the museum, the mountain, the theater, the boardroom, the high school, the hotel restaurant, and so forth. He has recounted, however, that this thematic inspiration soon began to intermingle with a different one, as "impulsions of a clearly formal nature" increasingly shaped his republican works. To understand these impulsions, a bit of history is necessary.

A Brief History of Constraint

In 1960, a conference was held at Cérisy-la-Salle entitled *Une nouvelle défense et illustration de la langue française* (modeled on Du Bellay's 1549 call for the enrichment of the French language). The conference was to honor the French man of arts and letters Raymond Queneau and, in particular, the colloquial richnesses he had discovered in such works as the recently published *Zazie in the Metro* (1959). This ten-day conference gave rise to one of the most curious French literary groups in a century rich in curious French literary groups—the *Ouvroir de littérature potentielle,* "Workshop of Potential Literature," or *Oulipo,* for short. The mathematicians and writers who made it up agreed to meet once a month. While not secret, the group was private, and went seven years before inducting a new member. As a young man, Queneau had been a Surrealist and like many a member left with the door slammed behind him. Informed by his experiences with the temperamental Breton and others in his Surrealist republic, Queneau decided, along with cofounder François Le Lionnais, that there would be no exclusions from the group—the maximum that would be allowed would be "excused absences" for those who passed away. Queneau and Le Lionnais themselves now hold such exemptions— as do Marcel Duchamp, Georges Perec, Italo Calvino, and others.[4]

Jacques Jouet was thirteen at the time of Oulipo's founding and thus ineligible for entry. By 1983 things had changed and Jouet found himself invited into the amicable circle that Oulipo

---

4   For an overview of Oulipo's activities, see *Oulipo: A Primer of Potential Literature*, edited by Warren Motte (Dalkey Archive, 1998) and the more recent *State of Constraint: New Work by Oulipo* (McSweeney's, 2006). As concerns Jouet, the reader is encouraged to consult Warren Motte's writings—particularly his "Jacques Jouet and the Literature of Exhaustion" (*SubStance*, Issue 96, 2001, 45–63).

still forms. But what did this mean? What does Oulipo do? Oulipo was formed not to compose literary *works*—this was something that its members believed writers could do well enough on their own. It was formed to compose literary *constraints*—constraints through which literary works might be written. Whether they *were* written or not was another question—and not the essential one. These constraints vary from the very simple to the very complex. The most famous case of the former is that of Georges Perec and his *La disparition* (The Disappearance[5])—a book of more than three hundred pages in which no word containing the letter *e* appears. To remain with that author, Perec's final novel, *La vie mode d'emploi* (*Life A User's Manual*), is a fine example of the latter, composed as it was through the constraints formed by the use of a complex algorithm

---

5   Translated into English as *A Void* (1994) by Gilbert Adair.

governing the recurrence of a whole network of objects, situations, themes, citations—and more.

As one expects from the member of such a group, Jouet has proven intensely interested in constraint. A work's "form," as he has often remarked, modifying a phrase from Francis Ponge, is "meaning's tautest string" (*la corde la plus tendue du sens*).⁶ For Jouet, this elegant formula expresses the relation of constraint to the work that it produces. Although a constraint might begin as something arbitrary and external to the work, it soon begins to inform and form its content. To say in this context then that form is "meaning's tautest string" is to say that the use of constraint is no sterile exercise in the manipulation of words, but is, instead, the setting of energizing obstacles, the composing of dynamic riddles for the writer to solve.

---

6   Ponge's remark concerned classicism, which he called, "la corde la plus tendue du baroque," the tautest string of the Baroque. In *Pour un Malherbe* (Paris: Gallimard, 1965, 238).

Such riddles are not, of course, foreign to Jouet's republic. In a work not yet translated, *Fins* (Ends), two Parisian couples pull meaning's string in a variety of ways. The first way is in a formal constraint that governs the book's division into paragraphs. It is based on one of the most time-honored and difficult constraints in Western poetry—the sestina (a form that involves the regular permutations of six rhymes). In *Fins*, the recurrent elements are not rhymes but sentences. The novel contains 216 paragraphs, each of which is composed of between one and six sentences. The first paragraph contains one sentence, the second two, the third three, and so forth, through the sixth paragraph. In the seventh paragraph, another permutation begins, in which the order is shifted. The pattern is followed until the exhaustion of all of the combinatorial possibilities ($6 \times 6 \times 6 = 216$). And it is here that meaning's taut string begins to resonate. This formal constraint

engenders a semantic one. Jouet's fellow Oulipian Calvino famously wrote a work consisting of
only the beginnings of a series of stories.[7] Each
of the 216 paragraphs in *Fins,* while fitting into
the larger story of which they are a part, is composed as an *ending* to the brief narrative which
that paragraph traces.

What, then, of *Upstaged*? Was it written in
response to a constraint? If so, what is it? *Or,* if
so, do we need to know it? Oulipians have been
of two minds on this matter, disagreeing as to
whether it was better to share the constraint
with the reader, as Perec and Calvino believed,
or, as Queneau argued, to remove the scaffold-
ing once you're done with the building. For some
cases, like that of *Fins,* Jouet has chosen to tell
his reader how he reached his ends. In a brief afterword to that work entitled, "To the Formalist

---

7   This novel is *If on a winter's night a traveler* (1979), whose
working title was *Incipit.*

Reader (Without the Author Formalizing Himself)," Jouet notes, "I made his book with many obscure things and two formal axioms."[8] *Upstaged* is graced with no similar afterword and leaves its reader in the dark as to the role constraint played in its composition.

Whereas *Fins* and *Annette et l'Etna* are then clearly Oulipian works pulled tight with the strings of constraint, *Mountain R* and *Upstaged* are of more uncertain character. This, however, does not mean that constraint plays no role in *Upstaged*. Whether or not formal axioms were employed in its writing, it is clear that it has much to say about constraint—and that it even offers something like an allegory of constraint. As the reader soon sees, it is a story about the strange

---

8   Jacques Jouet. *Fins.* Paris: P.O.L, 1999, 119. As concerns one of those formal axioms, it bears noting that the sestina has played an important role in a number of Oulipian constraints—seen with special refinement in Jacques Roubaud's *Hortense* novels and in Hervé Le Tellier's *The Sextine Chapel.*

fruits of the unexpected. A stranger arrives and his first act is, well, constraint (tying an actor to a chair). His next one is to oblige the troupe to follow his unexpected leads onstage. The ultimate effect of his imposition is liberatory. A walking, talking—and dashing—*clinamen*, the man they call the Usurper displaces the orderly fall of dramaturgical atoms. He functions as a spur to innovation, an opponent of settled thinking and acting. Constrained to improvise, the actors are removed from a rut they didn't realize they were in. Deprived of their routines, they discover new possibilities. Each reacts in his or her fashion. One faints, another falls in love. Roles are exchanged and the game of musical chairs they play sends the author onstage where he must come to terms with his actors' demands (one of which being that he commit suicide).

But, on another level, the Usurper *lifts* an important constraint: the play itself. For the actor, the play is pure constraint. Instead of speaking their mind, giving free rein to their feelings, following the unexpected turns of heart and mind—that they were born and will die, that they loved a girl with freckles and red hair, that they dream nightly of panda bears with frightening grins—they recite their lines. One way of looking at the stage is: constraints as far as the eye can see, and the French term for rehearsal—*repetition*—reinforces this idea. And yet, there is at the same time immeasurable room for diversity in the unity formed by a play. This is indeed the glory of the stage—the fine lines of individual interpretation traced by those who give it life. The actor must walk four paces to the settee and say, "But my dear, that simply will not do!" But *how* one takes those paces and says those lines can make a world of difference. In other words, the stage is the place where freedom and constraint meet and merge, and the reason that life in the theater shuttles back and forth between repetition and novelty. In

Upstaged, the pendulum swings wildly in the direction of novelty. And then it swings back.

In the light cast by novelty and constraint, the play's final line—"Never again!"—appears particularly rich. Spoken by "the President of the Republican Council," it closes the proceedings and serves as a menacing promise: never again will he allow such an assault on his presidential dignity. Spoken by the actor, it means: never again will he be bound and gagged, knocked unconscious, robbed of his role. Spoken as a member of the troupe, it means: never again will he be cowed by their "debonair dictator," the author-director Flavy. And, finally, spoken as a privileged witness to the night's drama, it means that what the audience saw was utterly unique, one of a kind, *never again* to be repeated.

Returning to republican matters, the upstaged actors at the end of this novel wonder whether they have witnessed a political statement—and Jouet's readers might find themselves in the same position in *Upstaged,* in *Mountain R,* and the rest of *La République roman.* In his *Raymond Queneau,* Jouet says of the young writer—in 1927, then a member of the Surrealists—"Queneau shows a clear apolitical bent even at a time when he is, to all appearances, quite politicized."[9] While this is an excellent description of Queneau's works and days, it might with equal justice be applied to Jouet's own development. It would be wrong to conclude that Jouet's works are primarily political ones. Upon closer inspection, one sees that he is far less interested in denouncing the *Irrépublique,* as he at one point calls it, or bringing about *une nouvelle République réembastillée,* as he remarks elsewhere, than in exploring the literary freedoms and constraints that a fictional republic offers.

---

9   Jacques Jouet. *Raymond Queneau.* Lyon: La Manufacture, 1988, 14.

Vladimir Nabokov, a lover of novels and puzzles, once said that "a great writer's world" is "a magic democracy where even some very minor character, even the most incidental character . . . has the right to live and breed." In the case of Jacques Jouet, we might modify this formula to say that what Jouet's works form is a magic *republic* where good actors and bad politicians, good daughters and bad fathers, mysterious mountain climbers and secretive curators all have an inalienable and enlightening right to live and breed.

LELAND DE LA DURANTAYE

JACQUES JOUET was elected to the Oulipo in 1983. He is the author of more than sixty texts in a variety of genres—novels, poetry, plays, literary criticism, and short fiction—including the novel *Mountain R*, which is part of his *La République roman* cycle, and was published by Dalkey Archive in 2004.

LELAND DE LA DURANTAYE is the Gardner Cowles Associate Professor of English at Harvard University. He is the author of *Style is Matter: The Moral Art of Vladimir Nabokov* (2007) and *Giorgio Agamben: A Critical Introduction* (2009).

SELECTED DALKEY ARCHIVE PAPERBACKS

PETROS ABATZOGLOU, *What Does Mrs. Freeman Want?*
MICHAL AJVAZ, *The Golden Age.*
The Other City.
PIERRE ALBERT-BIROT, *Grabinoulor.*
YUZ ALESHKOVSKY, *Kangaroo.*
FELIPE ALFAU, *Chromos.*
Locos.
IVAN ÂNGELO, *The Celebration.*
The Tower of Glass.
DAVID ANTIN, *Talking.*
ANTÓNIO LOBO ANTUNES, *Knowledge of Hell.*
ALAIN ARIAS-MISSON, *Theatre of Incest.*
IFTIKHAR ARIF AND WAQAS KHWAJA, EDS., *Modern Poetry of Pakistan.*
JOHN ASHBERY AND JAMES SCHUYLER, *A Nest of Ninnies.*
GABRIELA AVIGUR-ROTEM, *Heatwave and Crazy Birds.*
HEIMRAD BÄCKER, *transcript.*
DJUNA BARNES, *Ladies Almanack.*
Ryder.
JOHN BARTH, *LETTERS.*
Sabbatical.
DONALD BARTHELME, *The King.*
Paradise.
SVETISLAV BASARA, *Chinese Letter.*
RENÉ BELLETTO, *Dying.*
MARK BINELLI, *Sacco and Vanzetti Must Die!*
ANDREI BITOV, *Pushkin House.*
ANDREJ BLATNIK, *You Do Understand.*
LOUIS PAUL BOON, *Chapel Road.*
My Little War.
Summer in Termuren.
ROGER BOYLAN, *Killoyle.*
IGNÁCIO DE LOYOLA BRANDÃO, *Anonymous Celebrity.*
The Good-Bye Angel.
Teeth under the Sun.
Zero.
BONNIE BREMSER, *Troia: Mexican Memoirs.*
CHRISTINE BROOKE-ROSE, *Amalgamemnon.*
BRIGID BROPHY, *In Transit.*
MEREDITH BROSNAN, *Mr. Dynamite.*
GERALD L. BRUNS, *Modern Poetry and the Idea of Language.*
EVGENY BUNIMOVICH AND J. KATES, EDS., *Contemporary Russian Poetry: An Anthology.*
GABRIELLE BURTON, *Heartbreak Hotel.*
MICHEL BUTOR, *Degrees.*
Mobile.
Portrait of the Artist as a Young Ape.
G. CABRERA INFANTE, *Infante's Inferno.*
Three Trapped Tigers.
JULIETA CAMPOS, *The Fear of Losing Eurydice.*
ANNE CARSON, *Eros the Bittersweet.*
ORLY CASTEL-BLOOM, *Dolly City.*
CAMILO JOSÉ CELA, *Christ versus Arizona.*
The Family of Pascual Duarte.
The Hive.
LOUIS-FERDINAND CÉLINE, *Castle to Castle.*
Conversations with Professor Y.
London Bridge.
Normance.
North.
Rigadoon.
HUGO CHARTERIS, *The Tide Is Right.*
JEROME CHARYN, *The Tar Baby.*
ERIC CHEVILLARD, *Demolishing Nisard.*
MARC CHOLODENKO, *Mordechai Schamz.*
JOSHUA COHEN, *Witz.*
EMILY HOLMES COLEMAN, *The Shutter of Snow.*
ROBERT COOVER, *A Night at the Movies.*
STANLEY CRAWFORD, *Log of the S.S. The Mrs Unguentine.*
Some Instructions to My Wife.
ROBERT CREELEY, *Collected Prose.*
RENÉ CREVEL, *Putting My Foot in It.*
RALPH CUSACK, *Cadenza.*
SUSAN DAITCH, *L.C.*
Storytown.
NICHOLAS DELBANCO, *The Count of Concord.*
Sherbrookes.
NIGEL DENNIS, *Cards of Identity.*
PETER DIMOCK, *A Short Rhetoric for Leaving the Family.*
ARIEL DORFMAN, *Konfidenz.*
COLEMAN DOWELL, *The Houses of Children.*
Island People.
Too Much Flesh and Jabez.
ARKADII DRAGOMOSHCHENKO, *Dust.*
RIKKI DUCORNET, *The Complete Butcher's Tales.*
The Fountains of Neptune.
The Jade Cabinet.
The One Marvelous Thing.
Phosphor in Dreamland.
The Stain.
The Word "Desire."
WILLIAM EASTLAKE, *The Bamboo Bed.*
Castle Keep.
Lyric of the Circle Heart.
JEAN ECHENOZ, *Chopin's Move.*
STANLEY ELKIN, *A Bad Man.*
Boswell: A Modern Comedy.
Criers and Kibitzers, Kibitzers and Criers.
The Dick Gibson Show.
The Franchiser.
George Mills.
The Living End.
The MacGuffin.
The Magic Kingdom.
Mrs. Ted Bliss.
The Rabbi of Lud.
Van Gogh's Room at Arles.
ANNIE ERNAUX, *Cleaned Out.*
LAUREN FAIRBANKS, *Muzzle Thyself.*
Sister Carrie.
LESLIE A. FIEDLER, *Love and Death in the American Novel.*
JUAN FILLOY, *Op Oloop.*
GUSTAVE FLAUBERT, *Bouvard and Pécuchet.*
KASS FLEISHER, *Talking out of School.*
FORD MADOX FORD, *The March of Literature.*
JON FOSSE, *Aliss at the Fire.*
Melancholy.
MAX FRISCH, *I'm Not Stiller.*
Man in the Holocene.

FOR A FULL LIST OF PUBLICATIONS, VISIT:
www.dalkeyarchive.com

SELECTED DALKEY ARCHIVE PAPERBACKS

CARLOS FUENTES, *Christopher Unborn.*
Distant Relations.
Terra Nostra.
Where the Air Is Clear.
JANICE GALLOWAY, *Foreign Parts.*
The Trick Is to Keep Breathing.
WILLIAM H. GASS, *Cartesian Sonata
and Other Novellas.*
Finding a Form.
A Temple of Texts.
The Tunnel.
Willie Masters' Lonesome Wife.
GÉRARD GAVARRY, *Hoppla! 1 2 3.*
Making a Novel.
ETIENNE GILSON,
The Arts of the Beautiful.
Forms and Substances in the Arts.
C. S. GISCOMBE, *Giscome Road.*
Here.
Prairie Style.
DOUGLAS GLOVER, *Bad News of the Heart.*
The Enamoured Knight.
WITOLD GOMBROWICZ,
A Kind of Testament.
KAREN ELIZABETH GORDON,
The Red Shoes.
GEORGI GOSPODINOV, *Natural Novel.*
JUAN GOYTISOLO, *Count Julian.*
Exiled from Almost Everywhere.
Juan the Landless.
Makbara.
Marks of Identity.
PATRICK GRAINVILLE, *The Cave of Heaven.*
HENRY GREEN, *Back.*
Blindness.
Concluding.
Doting.
Nothing.
JIŘÍ GRUŠA, *The Questionnaire.*
GABRIEL GUDDING,
Rhode Island Notebook.
MELA HARTWIG, *Am I a Redundant
Human Being?*
JOHN HAWKES, *The Passion Artist.*
Whistlejacket.
ALEKSANDAR HEMON, ED.,
Best European Fiction.
AIDAN HIGGINS, *A Bestiary.*
Balcony of Europe.
Bornholm Night-Ferry.
Darkling Plain: Texts for the Air.
Flotsam and Jetsam.
Langrishe, Go Down.
Scenes from a Receding Past.
Windy Arbours.
KEIZO HINO, *Isle of Dreams.*
KAZUSHI HOSAKA, *Plainsong.*
ALDOUS HUXLEY, *Antic Hay.*
Crome Yellow.
Point Counter Point.
Those Barren Leaves.
Time Must Have a Stop.
NAOYUKI II, *The Shadow of a Blue Cat.*
MIKHAIL IOSSEL AND JEFF PARKER, EDS.,
*Amerika: Russian Writers View the
United States.*
GERT JONKE, *The Distant Sound.*
Geometric Regional Novel.
Homage to Czerny.
The System of Vienna.

JACQUES JOUET, *Mountain R.*
Savage.
Upstaged.
CHARLES JULIET, *Conversations with
Samuel Beckett and Bram van
Velde.*
MIEKO KANAI, *The Word Book.*
YORAM KANIUK, *Life on Sandpaper.*
HUGH KENNER, *The Counterfeiters.*
*Flaubert, Joyce and Beckett:
The Stoic Comedians.*
Joyce's Voices.
DANILO KIŠ, *Garden, Ashes.*
A Tomb for Boris Davidovich.
ANITA KONKKA, *A Fool's Paradise.*
GEORGE KONRAD, *The City Builder.*
TADEUSZ KONWICKI, *A Minor Apocalypse.*
The Polish Complex.
MENIS KOUMANDAREAS, *Koula.*
ELAINE KRAF, *The Princess of 72nd Street.*
JIM KRUSOE, *Iceland.*
EWA KURYLUK, *Century 21.*
EMILIO LASCANO TEGUI, *On Elegance
While Sleeping.*
ERIC LAURRENT, *Do Not Touch.*
HERVÉ LE TELLIER, *The Sextine Chapel.*
*A Thousand Pearls (for a Thousand
Pennies)*
VIOLETTE LEDUC, *La Bâtarde.*
EDOUARD LEVÉ, *Suicide.*
SUZANNE JILL LEVINE, *The Subversive
Scribe: Translating Latin
American Fiction.*
DEBORAH LEVY, *Billy and Girl.*
*Pillow Talk in Europe and Other
Places.*
JOSÉ LEZAMA LIMA, *Paradiso.*
ROSA LIKSOM, *Dark Paradise.*
OSMAN LINS, *Avalovara.*
The Queen of the Prisons of Greece.
ALF MAC LOCHLAINN,
The Corpus in the Library.
Out of Focus.
RON LOEWINSOHN, *Magnetic Field(s).*
MINA LOY, *Stories and Essays of Mina Loy.*
BRIAN LYNCH, *The Winner of Sorrow.*
D. KEITH MANO, *Take Five.*
MICHELINE AHARONIAN MARCOM,
The Mirror in the Well.
BEN MARCUS,
The Age of Wire and String.
WALLACE MARKFIELD,
Teitlebaum's Window.
To an Early Grave.
DAVID MARKSON, *Reader's Block.*
Springer's Progress.
Wittgenstein's Mistress.
CAROLE MASO, *AVA.*
LADISLAV MATEJKA AND KRYSTYNA
POMORSKA, EDS.,
*Readings in Russian Poetics:
Formalist and Structuralist Views.*
HARRY MATHEWS,
*The Case of the Persevering Maltese:
Collected Essays.*
Cigarettes.
The Conversions.
*The Human Country: New and
Collected Stories.*
The Journalist.

FOR A FULL LIST OF PUBLICATIONS, VISIT:
www.dalkeyarchive.com

ARNO SCHMIDT, *Collected Novellas.*
  Collected Stories.
  Nobodaddy's Children.
  Two Novels.
ASAF SCHURR, *Motti.*
CHRISTINE SCHUTT, *Nightwork.*
GAIL SCOTT, *My Paris.*
DAMION SEARLS, *What We Were Doing*
  and Where We Were Going.
JUNE AKERS SEESE,
  Is This What Other Women Feel Too?
  What Waiting Really Means.
BERNARD SHARE, *Inish.*
  Transit.
AURELIE SHEEHAN,
  Jack Kerouac Is Pregnant.
VIKTOR SHKLOVSKY, *Bowstring.*
  Knight's Move.
  A Sentimental Journey:
  Memoirs 1917–1922.
  Energy of Delusion: A Book on Plot.
  Literature and Cinematography.
  Theory of Prose.
  Third Factory.
  Zoo, or Letters Not about Love.
CLAUDE SIMON, *The Invitation.*
PIERRE SINIAC, *The Collaborators.*
JOSEF ŠKVORECKÝ, *The Engineer of*
  Human Souls.
GILBERT SORRENTINO,
  Aberration of Starlight.
  Blue Pastoral.
  Crystal Vision.
  Imaginative Qualities of Actual
  Things.
  Mulligan Stew.
  Pack of Lies.
  Red the Fiend.
  The Sky Changes.
  Something Said.
  Splendide-Hôtel.
  Steelwork.
  Under the Shadow.
W. M. SPACKMAN,
  The Complete Fiction.
ANDRZEJ STASIUK, *Fado.*
GERTRUDE STEIN,
  Lucy Church Amiably.
  The Making of Americans.
  A Novel of Thank You.
LARS SVENDSEN, *A Philosophy of Evil.*
PIOTR SZEWC, *Annihilation.*
GONÇALO M. TAVARES, *Jerusalem.*
  Learning to Pray in the Age of
  Technology.
LUCIAN DAN TEODOROVICI,
  Our Circus Presents . . .
STEFAN THEMERSON, *Hobson's Island.*
  The Mystery of the Sardine.
  Tom Harris.
JOHN TOOMEY, *Sleepwalker.*
JEAN-PHILIPPE TOUSSAINT,
  The Bathroom.
  Camera.
  Monsieur.
  Running Away.
  Self-Portrait Abroad.
  Television.
DUMITRU TSEPENEAG,
  Hotel Europa.

  The Necessary Marriage.
  Pigeon Post.
  Vain Art of the Fugue.
ESTHER TUSQUETS, *Stranded.*
DUBRAVKA UGRESIC,
  Lend Me Your Character.
  Thank You for Not Reading.
MATI UNT, *Brecht at Night.*
  Diary of a Blood Donor.
  Things in the Night.
ÁLVARO URIBE AND OLIVIA SEARS, EDS.,
  Best of Contemporary Mexican
  Fiction.
ELOY URROZ, *Friction.*
  The Obstacles.
LUISA VALENZUELA, *Dark Desires and*
  the Others.
  He Who Searches.
MARJA-LIISA VARTIO,
  The Parson's Widow.
PAUL VERHAEGHEN, *Omega Minor.*
BORIS VIAN, *Heartsnatcher.*
LLORENÇ VILLALONGA, *The Dolls' Room.*
ORNELA VORPSI, *The Country Where No*
  One Ever Dies.
AUSTRYN WAINHOUSE, *Hedyphagetica.*
PAUL WEST,
  Words for a Deaf Daughter & Gala.
CURTIS WHITE,
  America's Magic Mountain.
  The Idea of Home.
  Memories of My Father Watching TV.
  Monstrous Possibility: An Invitation
  to Literary Politics.
  Requiem.
DIANE WILLIAMS, *Excitability:*
  Selected Stories.
  Romancer Erector.
DOUGLAS WOOLF, *Wall to Wall.*
  Ya! & John-Juan.
JAY WRIGHT, *Polynomials and Pollen.*
  The Presentable Art of Reading
  Absence.
PHILIP WYLIE, *Generation of Vipers.*
MARGUERITE YOUNG, *Angel in the Forest.*
  Miss MacIntosh, My Darling.
REYOUNG, *Unbabbling.*
VLADO ŽABOT, *The Succubus.*
ZORAN ŽIVKOVIĆ, *Hidden Camera.*
LOUIS ZUKOFSKY, *Collected Fiction.*
SCOTT ZWIREN, *God Head.*